This Walker book
belongs to:

_____

_____

Don't swap
for fish
that are still
in the sea.

– old sailor saying

To the faculty, staff, and children of Shaaray Tefila Nursery School

First published 2016 by Walker Books Ltd, 87 Vauxhall Walk, London SE11 5HJ • This edition published 2017 • © 2016 Steve Light • The right of Steve Light to be identified as author/illustrator of this work has been asserted by him in accordance with the Copyright, Designs and Patents Act 1988 • This book has been typeset in Stempel Schneidler • Printed in China • 10 9 8 7 6 5 4 3 2 1

SWAP!

STEVE LIGHT

WALKER BOOKS
AND SUBSIDIARIES
LONDON · BOSTON · SYDNEY · AUCKLAND

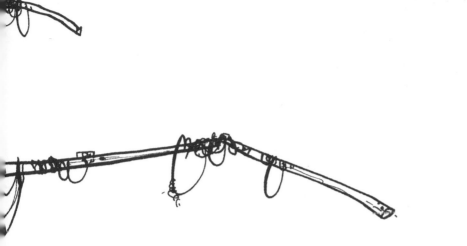

An old ship.

A sad friend.

A button ...

an idea.

One button for
two teacups.
SWAP!

Two teacups for
three coils of rope.

SWAP!

Two coils of rope
for six oars.

SWAP!

Two oars for four flags.

SWAP!

One flag for three anchors.

SWAP!

Two anchors for nine sails.

SWAP!

Two sails for
two ship's wheels.

SWAP!

One ship's wheel for three hats.

One hat for three birds.

SWAP!

One bird for
one carved figurehead.

SWAP!

A new ship.
A happy friend.

STEVE LIGHT is the author-illustrator of many books for children,
including *Have You Seen My Dragon?*, *Have You Seen My Monster?*
and *Lucky Lazlo*. When he is not writing or illustrating books, he teaches
at a nursery school. Steve lives in New York City with his wife and cat.

About *Swap!*, he says, "I love the idea of trading something small,
like a button, to acquire great fortune. Maybe it's because I grew
up rummaging for treasure in flea markets."

Find him online at **stevelightart.com** and on Twitter as **@SteveLight**.

Look out for:

978-1-4063-6063-9

"One of the most beautiful
counting books in a long
time" *Independent*

978-1-4063-7426-1

978-1-4063-6594-8

"Not since *Where the Wild Things
Are* has the monstrous had such
an appeal" *The Times*

Available from all good booksellers

www.walker.co.uk